ONCE A PONY TIME

AT CHINCOTEAGUE

By Lynne N. Lockhart & Barbara M. Lockhart
Illustrated by Lynne N. Lockhart

Mrs. Emory always felt fluttery when she first caught sight of the glimmering ocean and the crashing waves on the other side of the sand dunes.

"Oh, I just love the beach!" she sang out to Mr. Emory, who was trudging along behind her carrying the beach chairs. "Assateague is my favorite place. Maybe I'll even find some good shells today," she said.

"Right here's a good spot for our blanket, don't you think?" Mr. Emory asked her.

He had put up the beach chairs and Mrs. Emory had just spread out the blanket when they saw five ponies gallop past them. The ponies stopped suddenly by the water's edge and stood very still except for their swishing tails.

"Aren't they a pretty sight, dear?" said Mrs. Emory.

Mr. Emory nodded as he reached for his camera and walked toward the ponies.

But just as he was about to press the button for the picture, the ponies began to move about.

One followed the other as they came toward Mr. Emory. He backed up, still holding his camera in position.

The first pony, a stallion, walked right past him to the beach blanket. He didn't bother about Mrs. Emory sitting in the beach chair, but began nuzzling the picnic basket until it toppled over.

"I guess he's hungry," said Mrs. Emory, who began to worry about the lunch she'd brought.

Two more ponies followed close behind, trampling the blanket and poking through the sandwiches and potato chip bags that fell out of the picnic basket. A mare and her baby stayed off to one side. The little filly rubbed against her mother and shook her head.

"I didn't know they liked tuna fish!" exclaimed Mr. Emory as he began clicking his camera while one of the ponies ate a sandwich.

"Just a minute! Don't do that!" Mrs. Emory shouted and laughed at the ponies. "Oh, see if you can get a picture of the mother and her baby!" she called to her husband, and Mr. Emory did.

In the next minute, the lifeguard came running and clapping his hands. "Go away!" he shouted. The ponies eyed the lifeguard as they meandered down to the sea again. There they stood, sleepy-eyed and facing the wind. The foal still stayed close to her mother's side.

"Soon the ponies will be rounded up," said the lifeguard. "Wednesday they will swim across the channel to Chincoteague for the Pony Penning and Firemen's Carnival."

"That's right," said Mr. Emory. "It's the last Wednesday in July every year, isn't it?"

"I think we should go!" said Mrs. Emory, who began to think how happy her grandchildren would be to have a pony of their own. "It might be fun to buy one, you know."

"Whoa!" said Mr. Emory. "Ponies have to be brushed and combed, watered, fed, exercised, and penned up where we live. Sounds like a lot of work to me."

"We'll get our grandchildren to help," said Mrs. Emory, and she began to look for shells. Mr. Emory walked with her and every once in a while they stopped to pick up a shell.

"Look at the color of this jingle shell, like pure gold! And—oh, look at this—a perfect angel wing!" cried Mrs. Emory. "The shells are always prettier at the beach where they sparkle in the sun," she said as she put a shell back on the sand so the next wave could wash it again.

"They belong here," said Mr. Emory, thinking about the hundreds of shells they had at home, overflowing all the buckets and arranged on all the tables, some even hanging in wind chimes in front of the windows.

"I just can't help looking, though," said Mrs. Emory. "You never know what you'll find!" And she and Mr. Emory went on down the beach, searching.

On Wednesday, the Emorys drove to Chincoteague Island while the early morning mist still nestled around the town.

"What time are the ponies going to swim across the channel?" they asked the man selling Chincoteague Pony Swim hats at the pony pen.

"They won't let 'em swim in a strong tide so we'll have to wait for the slack tide," he said.

"Slack tide?" asked Mrs. Emory.

"That's the fifteen minutes or so when the tide changes from coming in to going out and the water is still," he said. "Wanna buy a hat?"

Mr. Emory bought one for himself, while Mrs. Emory put on her big straw hat. People began to crowd around the pony pen, some carrying lawn chairs and coolers.

"T-shirts! T-shirts for sale! Pony T-shirts!" called a lady carrying a boxful.

Boats arrived, some lining up along the green buoys and some along the red buoys, leaving a big space in the middle for the pony swim.

A man on the loudspeaker said, "The first colt to reach the shore after the swim will be raffled off at the carnival

grounds. Get your tickets now. Five for one dollar! Only five for one dollar for the pony raffle!"

Mrs. Emory nudged Mr. Emory. "Let's get some," she said.

"But what if we win?" he asked.

"Then we'll have to figure something out," said Mrs. Emory, smiling. She waved her arm to a boy selling raffle tickets. "We'll take two dollars' worth," she said.

"We have numbers 34861 to 34870," she said to Mr. Emory, putting the tickets in her pocketbook.

Men on horseback entered the pony pen. "Now, don't forget," said one of them. "The first colt on shore gets this leather string tied around its neck."

The loudspeaker came on again. "Ladies and gentlemen, the ponies have left the pen on Assateague and are heading toward the shore. In a few minutes, they'll be in the water."

Suddenly the biggest boat sent off a signal of bright orange smoke.

"Here they come!" yelled Mr. Emory, looking through his binoculars.

Everyone cheered as the horses and their riders on the other side of the channel herded the ponies into the water.

"One hundred and forty ponies, ladies and gentlemen, will be here in a few minutes," yelled the announcer.

"I can hear them neighing," said Mrs. Emory.

Mr. Emory got his camera ready. Everyone shifted to the best position to see the ponies. Closer and closer they came.

At last they arrived—
two stallions first, and, right
behind them, the little
brown filly, with the mare
close behind.

"It's the same one we
saw on the beach!" Mrs.
Emory exclaimed. "The
very same one! I'm sure of
it!"

A man on horseback
dismounted. He slipped the
leather string around the
filly's neck and knotted it
tight.

"You're it," he said.
"You're the one for the
raffle." The pony
scampered back to her
mother, breathing hard
and dripping wet.

Suddenly the pen was filled with ponies. Mixed up from their swim, they were sorting themselves out. Mares were neighing to their foals and stallions were eyeing each other. Some ponies were eating the fresh green marsh grass; some were rubbing against each other and snorting. Occasionally a pony came right up to the fence to be petted.

"I like that black one over there," someone said.

"Mommy, can we have that brown one?" said a little girl.

"What happens now, dear?" asked Mrs. Emory.

"They'll let the ponies rest and then herd them through town to the carnival grounds," replied Mr. Emory.

"And then they'll have the raffle?" asked Mrs. Emory.

"Yes, the filly that was first will be raffled off today," he said. "And some of the other foals will be auctioned off tomorrow."

They watched the ponies for a while and then Mr. and Mrs. Emory walked along toward the carnival grounds. Mrs. Emory was planning.

"We could use the garage for a pony shed," she said. "We could keep the car in the driveway."

"We'd have to put up a fence," said Mr. Emory. "I'm afraid the filly wouldn't have much room to run."

"Hmmm," said Mrs. Emory.

Suddenly they heard the sound of horses' hooves behind them. The riders were herding the ponies through town. Mr. and Mrs. Emory and everyone else stepped aside to let them by. Afterward no one could say why it happened—maybe it was a horsefly that bit one of the stallions, or maybe it was the shiny blue ball mounted on a pedestal in one of the yards that startled them—but the ponies began to run! They knocked down the pink flamingoes and wooden sheep in the front yards and trampled through the flower beds. They broke off geraniums and knocked down bicycles. The horseback riders shouted and called and finally the herd of ponies headed toward the open gate of the carnival grounds.

"Thank goodness!" laughed Mrs. Emory. Mr. Emory helped her along.

Crowds of people moved toward the pen at the carnival grounds. Children were still picking out the ponies they would like to have and, all the while, Mrs. Emory was making pony plans.

"Maybe we could use that old bathtub for a watering trough," she said to Mr. Emory.

"Hmmm," said Mr. Emory.

The announcer began to call everyone for the raffle. "Last chance to buy a raffle ticket, folks. All the money goes to the Chincoteague Volunteer Fire Company! Bring that little filly on up here now. Let's see whose filly she's going to be!"

The wild-eyed filly was brought to the platform.

Two men had their arms around her neck and one held her down in back. She neighed and neighed.

"Well now, you have a choice if we draw your number. You can keep her or let her go back to Assateague, never to be sold. All right, let's see who gets her!" said the announcer. He shook the trash can that held all the ticket stubs.

The filly tried to buck and kick, the whites of her eyes wide. She neighed again, terrified of all the people. The men held her tight.

"The number is . . ."

Mrs. Emory clutched the tickets in her hand.

"34870! 34870, who's got 34870?" called the announcer.

"I knew it! We do! We do! Over here!" shouted Mrs. Emory, waving her arm.

"Come right on up here, lady. Let's check your ticket. Yup, that's it—34870. Okay! What do you want to do?" asked the announcer. "Take her home or let her go back to the island?"

Mr. Emory looked at the filly. He remembered how she looked when he saw her on the beach at Assateague. He remembered the waves splashing in and how the ponies stood end to end, swishing their tails to keep the horseflies away. He remembered the sun on their backs and the smell of the salt air. He looked at Mrs. Emory. She wasn't thinking

26

about the pony but about the jingle shells and the angel
wings that always looked their best on the beach, sparkling
at the water's edge and washed by the waves.

They both said it at the same time. "Let her go back!"

Mr. Emory winked at Mrs. Emory. The crowd cheered and
the announcer untied the leather string around the filly's neck.

On the day when the ponies that weren't sold swam back to Assateague, the Emorys drove to the channel to see them off. There stood the filly by her mother. Then all the ponies trotted into the water and began swimming. Mr. Emory watched through his binoculars until they reached the other shore. Then he passed the binoculars to Mrs. Emory. And through the glasses, Mrs. Emory saw the mare and the filly climb onto the opposite shore, their backs glistening in the sun.